Yado Malley

and the
Unicorn Rainbow Ball

Kimberly Joan's **Codes for Kids** series

KIMBERLY JOAN

LANIER PRESS

*To my mom and dad (Joan and Lindsey) —
two educators who raised me and taught me everything about love, discipline, and laughter. I love you!*

To my sister Karen—Family is forever! I love you, Candy!

To my dear, sweet Keith—Thank you for being amazing.

To Trish, Jeff, and Truck—the best friends in the world! Love you guys!

Special thanks to Denise Renee and Scott Mattson

**LANIER
PRESS** *an Imprint of
BookLogix*

Alpharetta, GA

ISBN: 978-1-6653-0041-4 - Paperback
ISBN: 978-1-6653-0042-1 - Hardcover
eISBN: 978-1-6653-0100-8 - ePub
eISBN: 978-1-6653-0101-5 - Mobi

Library of Congress Control Number: 2021902379

♾ Printed in the United States of America   0 2 1 8 2 1

This paper meets the requirements of ANSI/NISO Z39.48-1992 (Permanence of Paper)

ABOUT KIMBERLY JOAN'S CODES FOR KIDS SERIES

If you are new to Kimberly Joan's brand and books, let me introduce myself.

As a celebrity nanny for over fifteen years, I've seen it all: tantrums, sibling fights, laundry nightmares, inconsolable whining that happens for no reason, and more! The great thing is, I have a "code" for that. A code is a way to classify typical problematic behaviors kids exhibit and situations they get into. They are:

Code 11: Preparation for the Destination
Code 12: A Tantrum
Code 13: A Full-On Tantrum
Code 14: Let It Go
Code 15: Sippy Cup is Community Property
Code 16: Get in Where you Fit in
Code 17: Someone is Not Playing Well with Others
Code 18: Laundry Drama
Code 19: The Witching Hour
Code 20: Bedtime is a Solo Sport
Code 57/11: The S#*t Has Hit the Fan!

Each code has a recommended, kid-driven solution. Learn more about all the codes in my book, *The Drinking Nanny: Codes to Live By When the Kids Drive you to Drink*, available now on Amazon.

In Kimberly Joan's Codes for Kids series, I share child-friendly stories that help them learn better ways to handle conflicts and situations they often find themselves in.

Each book shows a different code in action. This story, *Yado Malley and the Unicorn Rainbow Ball*, highlights Code 17. It will show how to get along with friends or siblings. So snuggle up and invite your child to read along.

This is yado Malley. He is five years old.
yado loves going to school and being in MS. Henry's kindergarten class.

Recess is yado's favorite time of day. It's when he and his
friends play lots of fun games with different toys.

But there is one very special toy that everyone loves best
. . . the unicorn Rainbow Ball!

No other ball is like the unicorn Rainbow Ball! It is the color of a sparkly rainbow. The unicorn Rainbow Ball lights up when it bounces! And it can bounce super-duper high!

The unicorn Rainbow Ball is so cool that its unicorn horn disappears when it bounces. Then, the horn reappears when it is resting.

What makes the unicorn Rainbow Ball even more special is that it can play any game!

Lucy and Henry love to play basketball with the unicorn Rainbow Ball.

Kathleen and Augusta enjoy playing foursquare with the unicorn Rainbow Ball.

Amelia and Adair even jump rope with the unicorn Rainbow Ball.

The unicorn Rainbow Ball is truly magical!

Because everyone loves playing with the Unicorn Rainbow Ball, MS. Henry keeps it in a special bin, away from the other recess toys. But she always makes sure everyone has a chance to play with the Unicorn Rainbow Ball.

Today, before they go outside for recess, Ms. Henry reviews the playground rules with the class.

"Who can tell me what we should do when we go outside?" she asks in a kind voice.

"Share, care, and have fun!" they all answer.

"Very good, class!" Ms. Henry says proudly.

"Today, it is Amelia and Adair's turn to play with the unicorn Rainbow Ball for the first five minutes. After that, we will all take turns sharing the ball so that everyone will have a turn. Remember, sharing is caring. Are we ready to go outside?"

The class replies in unison, "Yes, Ms. Henry!"

yado and his friends file into two straight lines quietly.

"Now remember," Ms. Henry reminds them. "If I see any code-worthy behavior, we will take time out to work it out. Okay?"

Twenty little heads nod.

"Great! Let's have some fun!"

Ms. Henry swings the doors open into the bright sunlight, and
the sound of cheerful playing quickly fills the yard.

Yado races to the swings and gets one! After a few minutes, he moves on to the
slide. Just as he lands, something across the yard catches his attention.

It's the unicorn Rainbow Ball lying on the ground, all by itself!
Amelia and Adair's five minutes must already be up.

yado takes off running! He pumps his legs and arms as he tries to grab the unicorn Rainbow Ball before anyone else can.

But just as he puts his hands on the ball, someone else's hands are there too. It's his best friend, Tuck. Tuck snatches up the unicorn Rainbow Ball and starts to run away.

14

"Hey!" Yado yells. "Give it back! I had it first!"

"No you didn't! I picked it up first, so I get to play with it now," Tuck says over his shoulder.

"Nooooooo!" Yado squeals. He catches up to Tuck and reaches out to grab the unicorn Rainbow Ball.

As the boys wrestle, they fall on the ground, both tightly gripping the unicorn Rainbow Ball.

Suddenly, Ms. Henry appears.

Code 17

Not Playing Well with Others

"Yado! Tuck!" She says sharply. "Are we having a Code 17? Do we need time out to work this out?"

Her voice startles Yado and Tuck. In their confusion, the unicorn Rainbow Ball pops out of their hands and bounces away.

But something really interesting happens . . .

When it bounces away, the unicorn Rainbow Ball lands on its unicorn horn. But instead of disappearing like it normally does, the unicorn horn acts like a super spring.

It causes the unicorn Rainbow Ball to bounce so high into the sky that it lands on a cloud!

Papa Cloud hears the unicorn Rainbow Ball land with a sad puff.

"Hey there, unicorn Rainbow Ball!" Papa Cloud says in a kind voice.
"What are you doing all the way up here?"

"I'm sorry, Papa Cloud," replies the unicorn Rainbow Ball. "I needed to get away for a moment."

"You seem a little down. Do you want to talk about it?" Papa Cloud asks.

"Well, I'm so used to children being happy when I'm around that it makes me sad when they start fighting over me. I just want Yado and Tuck to work it out so we can all have fun together."

Papa Cloud is a good listener. He also gives good advice. "Running away doesn't solve anything. You have to give Yado and Tuck the chance to work it out."

"Do you really think they can?" the unicorn Rainbow Ball asks, perking up.

"Well," replies Papa Cloud, "there's only one way to find out!"

Papa Cloud tickles the unicorn Rainbow Ball, who starts giggling and wiggling uncontrollably. He rolls over onto his side and falls off the cloud.

As he falls through the sky on his way back down to the playground, Ms. Henry and the boys are talking it out.

"Boys, what's a Code 17?" MS. Henry asks.

Yado and Tuck look at each other sheepishly and mutter,
"Someone's not playing well with others."

"Should we fight over a toy we both want to play with?"

Yado fidgets with his fingers. Tuck looks down at the ground. They both shake their heads no.

"What is a different choice you could have made?" Ms. Henry guides.

"Well," Tuck starts slowly, "I did see yado running toward the ball. I didn't have to snatch it up first."

"And I didn't have to try to pull the ball out of your hands," yado confesses. "I'm sorry, Tuck."

"I'm Sorry, too, yado!" Tuck hugs his friend.

"Boys, that is very kind of you both!" Ms. Henry beams. "By the way, where is the Unicorn Rainbow Ball?"

At just that moment, the Unicorn Rainbow Ball lands back on the ground behind them with a soft *plop-plop-plop!*

yado and Tuck turn around at the same time and take off running for the ball. They both pick it up at the same time, but this time, they don't fight.

Instead, yado says, "Hey Tuck! Why don't we come up with a game we can play together? That way we both get to have fun!"

"yeah!" Tuck yelps in excitement.

28

And just like that, the Code 17 is over. Yado and Tuck play kindly with each other until recess is finished.

THE END

HEY YADO, WHAT DO YOU KNOW?

yado says . . .

"Today, I learned that if a friend and I both want to play with the same toy, we don't have to fight. We can either take turns playing or we can share and play together. What did you learn from this story?"

ABOUT THE AUTHOR

Kimberly Joan was born in Little Rock, Arkansas. She holds a bachelor of arts degree in history from the university of Arkansas at Pine Bluff. Kimberly Joan launched her career by working in daycares and public schools in Marietta and Atlanta, Georgia. She has been a private nanny to many families in Atlanta for over twenty-five years. Kimberly has also worked as a celebrity nanny and has been on many fun adventures through her work.

CPSIA information can be obtained
at www.ICGtesting.com
Printed in the USA
BVHW022348250521
608093BV00002B/33